THE MAGICAL NORTH POLE

TOM FLETCHER

Illustrated by SHANE DEVRIES

PUFFIN

PUFFIN BOOKS

UK | USA | Canada | Ireland | Australia
India | New Zealand | South Africa

Puffin Books is part of the Penguin Random House group of companies
whose addresses can be found at global.penguinrandomhouse.com.

www.penguin.co.uk   www.puffin.co.uk   www.ladybird.co.uk

Penguin
Random House
UK

Made for McDonald's 2020
001

Printed in China
THH A4C

A CIP catalogue record for this book is available from the British Library

ISBN: 978–0–241–43895–4

The National Literacy Trust is a registered charity no. 1116260 and a company limited
by guarantee no. 5836486 registered in England and Wales and a registered charity in
Scotland no. SC042944. Registered address: 68 South Lambeth Road, London SW8 1RL.
National Literacy Trust logo and reading tips copyright © National Literacy Trust, 2020
literacytrust.org.uk/donate

FSC
MIX
Paper
FSC® C017606

Meet Izzy and Benji.

They're just like you, except they have a
magical time-travelling van that can take them
to all kinds of amazing places! What Exciting
World will they go to this time . . . ?

You know that sound when your magical time-travelling van crashes into deep snow?

No? You don't have a magical time-travelling van?

Oh.

Well, it sounds something like this:

SSSSCCCCHHHWWWOOOOOOOSH!

In about seven pages, Izzy and her little cousin Benji will hear that sound. But, right now, they're lying against a tree in Izzy's garden, feeling very, very, VERY hot.

'I'm very, very, VERY hot,' said Izzy.

(I told you.)

She fanned herself with her hand. 'I wish we had a swimming pool,' she sighed.

Lots of her friends had gone on exciting holidays this summer, to places with pools and beaches and those cool drinks with colourful umbrellas. But Izzy's mum and dad had said that they couldn't afford to go away this year, so she and Benji were stuck at home in the garden. And it was **TOO HOT**!

3

'I'm hotter than a hot dog on the barbecue,' Izzy joked. But Benji didn't laugh.

Izzy looked at her little cousin. Normally on a summer's day Benji would be getting into all sorts of trouble, like climbing a tree and finding himself stuck halfway up. But now he had just flopped on to a branch.

'Do you think it's hot in Greece?' he asked.

Benji was staying with Izzy's family for six months while his mum worked in Greece, digging up old things. (She was an archaeologist, not a dog, although they both got very excited when they found a bone.)

Izzy knew that Benji must be missing his mum. Luckily, she also knew something that would cheer him up.

'*Do you want to go on an adventure?*' she
whispered.

'YES!' Benji leapt down from the tree
excitedly.

'Mum! We're going to play in the van!'
Izzy called.

'OK, Iz!' Mum called back.

I know what you're thinking. Yes, this *is* the van I was telling you about right at the start! It was parked on the driveway next to Izzy's garden. It used to belong to her grandpa, and it was very special indeed. It was special to Izzy because it reminded her of Gramps, whom she missed very much, and because it was exactly the same shade of blue as his warm, twinkly eyes. But it was **extra-specially special** for another secret reason: it could travel through time and space to all kinds of wondrously marvellous, marvellously wondrous places.

I know, right?

AMAZING!

And, once Izzy and Benji had been on their adventure, the van would bring them back to the very same second that they'd left, so Izzy's mum wouldn't even know they'd gone!

Izzy and Benji climbed in and buckled their seat belts. Then Izzy pressed a button to switch the van from Everyday mode to Exciting

Worlds mode, and started the engine. They were off! There was a *whoosh* of icy cold air – as if someone had opened a freezer – as the TimeFreeze700™ engine kicked in.

'*Oooh!*' Izzy and Benji said together, enjoying the deliciously cold air. There was a sound like ice cubes clinking through pipes, and the van began to move. Faster and faster and faster it went, until the houses around them were just blurs, and the scenery began to change from houses and cars to something

VAST

and cold

and empty

and white.

SSSSCCCCHHHWWWOOOOOOOSH!

The van crashed in the snow. (Just like I told you it would.)

Izzy and Benji peered out of the window. All they could see was white. Freezing cold white.

Izzy looked down at her dress and shoes. Benji was wearing shorts and a T-shirt, and was already shivering.

'Well, at least we're not going to be too hot any more,' Izzy said. 'Do you know where we are?'

'I can't tell!' Benji said, looking at the stark white nothing.

Suddenly Izzy spotted something glinting in the snow. She pushed open the van door, which was almost frozen shut with ice, and slowly put one foot down into the crunchy white snow, where it made a deep footprint. '*Brrrrrr!*' she said. 'Look, Benji, there's something here – it looks a bit like a golden thermometer . . .'

Benji jumped out next to her and stared at the strange object. It *did* look like a thermometer, with a line of glowing red liquid running up the middle. But what was it doing here? And where were they?

There was something almost magical about this snowy place . . .

Snow?

Magic?

And then Izzy had a brainwave.

'Benji . . .' she said, turning to him with her

eyes shining bright. 'You don't think we're at the North Pole, do you?'

Benji's mouth dropped open.

'That means . . .' Izzy continued.

'SANTA!' cried Benji.

And at that very moment . . .

POP!

Benji disappeared! Just like that. In the wink of a blink of an eye. One moment he was right there – a few millimetres from Izzy's face – and the next he was gone!

'Benji?' Izzy called, but her voice drifted on the frozen wind into the distant nothingness.

There was only snow as far as her eyes could see. All of a sudden, a gust of wind *whooshed*

past and Izzy thought she heard whispers.
'Benji?' she called again.

Izzy tried to think. Benji must have done
something to make himself disappear. But
what?

And then she knew.

'SANTA!' she yelled – and the most spectacularly magical thing happened. She didn't disappear like Benji had. Quite the opposite, in fact: EVERYTHING ELSE appeared. And, by EVERYTHING, I mean **EVERYTHING!** Suddenly Izzy was standing at the entrance to an enormous wooden building. A sign over the doorway said:

Izzy couldn't believe how grand it was. As she marvelled at the twisty turrets, the puffing chimneys, the toboggan-run path and the snowflake door knocker, her mouth dropped open in wonder.

'Hi, Izzy!' Benji said, grinning happily. He was now wearing a Christmas jumper with a dinosaur on it, a bobble hat and knitted slippers with curly toes. Izzy looked down and saw that her clothes had changed too, and she was deliciously warm and cosy in a snowflake coat.

Then Izzy realized that she and Benji were not alone. They were surrounded by a crowd of creatures. Small, strange, magical creatures!

Even though Izzy had never seen one before, she knew at once that these small creatures were elves!

'Hello, elves!' she said.

The elves all backed off, looking nervous.
Then one by one they popped out again,
looking frightened and cross, before all of a
sudden they started singing!

'Some kids are here! Some kids, it's true!
Oh, what are we poor elves to do?
They've seen our secret hiding spot
And everything has gone to pot!
We could not leave them there to freeze –
We heard them yelling on the breeze –

And so we brought them here today
But what will Santa think and say?
He'll soon be back from holiday!
He'll land here in his great red sleigh!
Quick! Turn around! Move out the way!
Santa's back, hip hip hooray!'

The elves stopped singing and stood back. Izzy and Benji spun round to see a gigantic red sleigh appear out of thin air above them, and circle down very fast towards where they were standing. The sleigh was even more incredible than Izzy could ever have dreamt it to be.

Shimmeringly shiny, ridonkulously red and

monstrously
massive!

But that wasn't the most wonderful thing about it. Most wonderful, Izzy thought, were the powerful creatures pulling it. She counted eight in total, striding through the air side by side, their antlers gleaming.

The flying reindeer!

'Whoa, whoa, whoa!' cried a deep, booming voice from overhead as the sleigh swooped round them and then touched down with a smooth *swish* along the snow. That's when Izzy first saw him. She couldn't believe her eyes. It was really him. Actually. Genuinely. One hundred per cent authentically. The real deal.

'SANTA!' Benji yelled again.

Santa pulled hard on the reins and the sleigh came to a stop directly in front of Izzy, Benji and the crowd of tiny elves that had gathered to greet him.

The elves rushed forward, cheering and screaming like crazed fans at a rock concert, but Izzy still had a perfect view of Santa as the elves were only half Benji's height! The mind-blowingly massive man stepped down from his sleigh. He wasn't wearing his famous red suit but blue shorts and a colourful Hawaiian shirt decorated with palm trees. On his head was a yellow baseball cap bearing the words HO HO HOLIDAY!

(That's right. Even Santa likes to have a summer holiday!)

Apart from his clothes, Santa looked every bit the jolly, happy man you would expect. But Izzy was worried. The elf song had made her feel naughty, as if she and Benji shouldn't be there! What would Santa do? What would he say?

She was about to find out.

Santa spotted something out of place – Izzy and Benji! 'What the crackers is *this*?' he asked, completely confuddled. He bounced straight over to where they were squished in the centre of a crowd of elves, and stood, towering impressively, over them. 'You're a little tall for an elf!' he said as Benji giggled delightedly. '*Why*, you're not an elf at all! Nor a skating snowman, nor a forest fairy, nor a reindeer!' He glanced at Izzy. 'Tell me, are you a mountain troll? Yes, I've heard of lost, wandering trolls

before, but never seen one. How fascinating!'
He rubbed his hands together excitedly.

'We're not trolls!' Izzy laughed.

Santa paused and scratched his beard
thoughtfully.

'No . . . of course you're not! Wait . . . don't
tell me . . . you're a . . . bald yeti! *Yes!* That's it.
How peculiar!'

'No!' Benji giggled. 'We're not one of those
either!'

'Hmmm, not a troll and not a bald
yeti, eh? Don't tell me! I'm thinking,
I'm thinking, I'm thinking . . .
Oh, what a fun guessing
game this is!'

Santa did a little hop and a skip and walked round Izzy and Benji, inspecting them.

'Santa!' Benji said politely. 'I'm not a troll or a yeti. I'm just a boy!'

There was a sudden rumble of whispers from the surrounding elves.

'*Just* a boy?' Santa bellowed in his mighty voice.

Izzy pulled Benji close. She was unsure if Santa was jolly happy or jolly angry.

'JUST a boy?' he repeated, and looked around at his elves. Then all of a sudden Santa seemed to find something completely hilarious.

'Ha-HA-HA! Ho-HO-HO!' He boomed an enormous laugh that made his belly ripple and

wobble. 'There's no such thing as JUST a boy!
Allow me to explain. You see, up here we have
all sorts of wonderfully magical creatures. But
there's something we don't have – the most
magical creatures in all the world . . .'

Izzy and Benji didn't have a clue what they
could be.

'Children!' Santa said with a smile.

'*Children?*' Izzy said. 'Children aren't magic. I'm a child and I'm not magic at all!'

All the elves giggled and Santa smiled knowingly.

'Oh, but you are! You really, truly are. You just don't know it! You can create impossible worlds in your imagination that don't really exist. *That* is magic. Because you can only see the best in people, the best in the world, in life. *That* is magic. Because you understand the importance of silliness, the importance of fun, of laughing and playing, which grown-ups have forgotten. *That* is magic. But, most of all, because you believe, without question, in the impossible. Without needing proof. Without hesitation. *That* is magic.'

Izzy couldn't believe what she was hearing. She could do all those things and she hadn't even realized that they were magic!

'Aha! And, speaking of belief, I see you have something of mine.' Santa pointed to the strange golden thermometer in Izzy's hand.

'Oh, is it yours, Santa? I found it in the snow!' Izzy explained, handing it over to the ginormous man.

'Well, butter my crumpets, what a stroke of luck! This is my beliefometer. I lost it a little

while ago, when I was out making a snow angel
in a fresh mound of snow. It must have fallen
out of my pocket! It's a very special instrument
that allows me and my elves to measure belief.'
He pointed to the glowing red line and
beamed. 'And it looks like the children of the
world still have plenty of belief! That's jolly
good news. You see, belief is the reason I am
able to exist . . . Izzy and Benji.'

At the mention of their names, Izzy couldn't help but notice that all the elves started whispering among themselves again.

'How do you know our names?' she asked. 'We haven't told you them.'

'Well, it took me a moment to realize who you were. I didn't expect to see any youngsters at the North Pole, you see. We haven't had children here for a very long time,' said Santa thoughtfully. 'But, now that you're here, why don't you come inside?' He opened his arms and stepped up to the enormous wooden doors of his Snow Ranch. 'Let's go!'

Santa led Izzy and Benji through some smaller, more sensibly sized doors that were cut

into the ridiculously large doors and they
entered the grandest entrance hall you could
possibly imagine.

You want to try? Go ahead!

Imagine **gigantic**,

quadruple-height ceilings . . .

Keep going . . .

A little taller than that.

Whoa!

Stop!

That's just silly! Bring them down a tad . . .
There! That looks about right.

The floors were made of huge slabs of
Christmas-tree pine that were as warm as a cup
of tea under your feet. That's because the
underfloor-heating system used actual English
breakfast tea to heat the pipes.

The air smelt of fresh *vaninnamon* (that's

vanilla and cinnamon mixed together), and the sounds of carols and pointless family bickering – the true sounds of Christmas – echoed from somewhere in the distance. Izzy and Benji couldn't believe their eyes, ears or noses.

'Come in, come in! Welcome to my home.' Santa grinned as he spun round merrily with his arms wide.

'This place is amazing!' Benji gasped.

'We have everything you could possibly imagine, and a few things you probably can't,' Santa said with a chuckle as he skipped down the wooden hallway of his supersized log cabin, its walls decorated with colourful drawings from children around the world. He did a little cartwheel and went into a forward roll, then pushed open heavy double doors leading to what looked like a library.

'Look at all the books!' Izzy cried.

'These aren't books – these are the lists,' Santa said, running his fingers over the ancient spines of thick tomes that lined every wall.

'You mean, *the* Nice List?' Izzy asked.

'And the Naughty one,' Santa replied, pointing to the opposite wall, which housed an equally daunting number of books.

Izzy laughed as Benji gave a little shudder. 'I hope I'm never on the Naughty List!' he said.

Santa led them to the library fireplace, where there were two big chairs next to a roaring fire. Santa sat on one and Izzy and Benji sat together on the other (the chairs were Santa-sized, so there was more than enough room for them both).

'Ah, it's good to be home, even though I did enjoy getting a bit of sunshine!' Santa said. He clicked his fingers, and suddenly he was dressed in his familiar red suit, with a black belt and buckle and a big red hat. He didn't seem to

notice that he was still wearing flip-flops.

'That's better!' he said. 'Now, Izzy and Benji – I only normally do this at Christmastime . . . but, since you've come all this way, I'd like to give you both a present.'

'*A present?*' Benji breathed.

'Why, yes!' Santa continued. 'Anything you like. This *is* the North Pole!'

He pressed a button and the library ceiling opened to reveal the night sky above.

'Wow!' Izzy and Benji gasped, and the elves all crowded into the room, chattering excitedly.

'The elves did it. It's a brilliant invention, but not terribly practical when it's snowing,' Santa whispered, with a wink.

The sky over their heads was filled with stars – and something else.

Beautiful blue, and flashes of green, purple

and yellow filled the air, dancing across
the sky.

The Northern Lights!

'This entire place is made from children's
dreams!' Santa told them. 'It's the one place
in the whole wide world where whatever you
truly desire can materialize before your very
eyes.'

'I know what I want!' Benji said. Instantly,
the lights high above his head formed into the

outline of a huge green dinosaur-shaped paddling pool.

Santa laughed. 'Done!'

'What is it?' Izzy asked. 'I don't see anything.'

Santa tapped the side of his nose. 'Ah, that's because it isn't your present,' he said. 'Now, what would you like, young Izzy?'

A present from Santa . . . anything she wanted . . . Izzy thought about it and looked up at the sky. There was one thing she wanted more than anything. She wanted Gramps back. But that couldn't happen, could it? Izzy stared upwards, holding her breath.

The North Pole had never been so quiet.

Smaller elves climbed on the shoulders of taller elves who were already standing on the very tallest elves to get a better view.

But nothing happened.

Santa's eyes stared deep into Izzy's. His kind face had a wise, knowing look, as though he already had the answer to every question you could possibly think of before you'd even thought of it.

COLOUR US iN!

'Oh, Izzy, I'm very sorry, but I'm afraid I can't do that . . .' said Santa in the kindest, deepest, wisest voice.

Izzy shook her head and tried not to cry. She knew that not even Christmas magic could bring Gramps back, but it was still what she wanted most.

'He's gone to the next adventure,' Santa said kindly. 'But he lives on in you and Benji – and in that very special van that's parked just outside. As long as you remember people, they're never truly gone.'

He placed his huge, warm hand on Izzy's shoulder. 'Izzy, close your eyes. Let's see if we can think of another gift, something to bring you joy and delight,' he said.

Izzy closed her eyes. Suddenly glorious music filled the air. A gramophone on a table next to the fire had burst into life on its own and was playing a beautiful song. Izzy opened her eyes and was surprised to see Santa and the elves all staring up at something. Something above her head.

'What is it?' Benji said, hopping about. 'I can't see!'

Izzy looked up, and what she saw completely took her breath away. The greens and blues, purples and yellows of the Northern Lights had been wondrously woven into a shape in the starry sky over the North Pole – it was her mum, her dad and Benji, and everyone was on holiday, having fun! Izzy could hardly take it all in.

Then, all of a sudden, the lights and colours started swaying and swirling around to the sound pouring from the gramophone, and in the sky Benji ran up to another figure and leapt into her arms. And there was Benji with his mum. Izzy thought how much her little cousin was missing his mum, and suddenly she knew exactly what she wanted.

Santa winked. 'It will be done,' he promised.

'Thank you, Santa,' she said with a smile.

As the Northern Lights flickered overhead, Izzy heard something else – the van's horn. It was time to go.

'But we just got here!' Benji complained.

'Oh!' all the elves sighed.

Two of them put their arms round Benji.

'Don't say you're leaving, no, not yet! Can't we keep him as our pet?'

Izzy looked around sadly. She would have loved to stay and explore more of the magical North Pole, but, if the van beeped three times, they'd be stuck here forever!

'We've got to go,' she said. 'Besides, I want my present!'

'What did you ask for?' Benji asked.

'Wait and see!' Izzy told him, smiling secretively.

Before they left, Santa gave them each a big hug. It was like falling into the squishiest armchair ever, one that was so deep you almost got stuck. Then they ran through the snow back to the van, all the elves following them and waving madly.

As they buckled their seat belts, Izzy stared at the amazing sight of the ranch, Santa and the elves for a moment longer before she started the engine. She never wanted to forget this

place! They waved and the whole ranch, with
Santa and the elves waving back at them,
disappeared.

Their Christmas outfits faded away, leaving
them in their summer clothes. But then the
cosy clothes reappeared, neatly folded on the

van's dashboard, with a note that said: *For your
next chilly adventure.*

They both sighed as the van whisked them
off and they landed with a bump back in Izzy's
driveway.

'That was just . . . magic!' Benji said happily.
'I can't wait for Christmas now!'

Izzy threw open the van's doors and the
sunshine poured over them like melted butter.
'Neither can I, but right now let's enjoy the
summer!' She grinned. It was nice to be warm
again!

'Izzy! Benji!'

Izzy's mum came running out of the house
with an excited shriek, flapping something in

the air. It looked like a letter. 'Guess what? I entered a competition, and I've won a family holiday to Greece! I can't believe it! We can go and visit your mum, Benji!'

Benji's eyes went wide. 'I can see Mum?' he gasped – then looked at Izzy. 'Your present! That's what you asked for!' He gave Izzy a tight hug and whispered, 'Thank you, Iz.'

'Oh, and there's something else that arrived for you two,'

Mum said, pointing to the back garden.

'What did you get? It better not be a dinosaur,' Izzy warned.

Benji gave an excited grin and they both ran to the back garden. There was an enormous paddling pool – and it was shaped like a dinosaur! Dad was filling it up with a hosepipe.

'We don't know who sent it to you. It just came with this postcard,' Mum said, looking confused.

Izzy and Benji took the postcard. On one side there was a picture of the swirling, swooping Northern Lights. On the other side it read: *Izzy and Benji, have a brilliant summer holiday!*

'You said you wanted to go swimming,' Benji said, shrugging as Izzy hugged him.

They ran upstairs to get changed into their swimsuits. Another adventure was over, but their summer fun had just begun!

RHYME TiME

Santa's elves always talk in rhymes, but they've got into a muddle! Can you help them by matching the rhyming words?

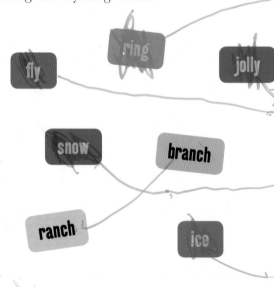

fly

ring

jolly

snow

branch

ranch

ice

callum

sleigh

sky

sing

yay

go

holly

nice

Turn to the last page for the answers.

HOLIDAY WISHES

If you could go on holiday anywhere, where
would you go? Use these pages to write about
your dream holiday.

el le unes dues tres
Cators cans desept
deswuet des nuf
vunt yan

CALLUM   MUM

MEGAN   MUM

Lauren   Dad.

SEMUN
WILLEAM
MEGHN
CÓLLUMA   MUM
AXEDAN   bab
LOREN

une   die   twa
caba   sank   sese
seft   whet   nng   dese

THE NORTHERN LIGHTS

Izzy and Benji see images dancing in the beautiful Northern Lights. Can you join the dots to find out what picture is in the sky?

Rudolph

Turn to the last page for the answer.

Izzy and Benji have travelled to the magical North Pole! Add stickers to this page to make an amazing Christmas scene.

RHYME TIME

sleigh — sky

fly — ring — jolly — sing — yay

snow — branch

ranch — ice — holly — nice

RUDOLPH

THE NORTHERN LIGHTS

RUDOLPH